The Tiger's Apprentice Trilogy

THE TIGER'S APPRENTICE, BOOK ONE

TIGER'S BLOOD, BOOK TWO

TIGER MAGIC, BOOK THREE

Dragon of the Lost Sea Fantasies

DRAGON OF THE LOST SEA

DRAGON STEEL

DRAGON CAULDRON

DRAGON WAR

Chinatown Mysteries

THE CASE OF THE GOBLIN PEARLS

THE CASE OF THE FIRECRACKERS

THE CASE OF THE LION DANCE

Edited by Laurence Yep

AMERICAN DRAGONS:

TWENTY-FIVE ASIAN VOICES

Awards

LAURA INGALLS WILDER AWARD

LAURENCE YEP

THE STAR MAKER

HARPER

An Imprint of HarperCollinsPublishers

Library of Congress Cataloging-in-Publication Data
Yep, Laurence.
    The star maker / by Laurence Yep. — 1st ed.
        p.   cm.
    Summary: With the help of his popular uncle Chester, a
young Chinese-American boy tries hard to fulfill a promise
to have firecrackers for everyone on the Chinese New Year
in 1954. Includes an afterword with information about the
Chinese customs portrayed in the story.
    Includes bibliographical references.
    ISBN 978-0-06-025315-8 (trade bdg.)
    ISBN 978-0-06-025316-5 (lib. bdg.)
    [1. Uncles—Fiction. 2. Family life—California—
San Francisco—Fiction. 3. Chinese New Year—Fiction.
4. Chinese Americans—Fiction. 5. Chinatown (San
Francisco, Calif.)—History—Fiction. 6. San Francisco
(Calif.)—History—20th century—Fiction.] I. Title.
PZ7.Y44Su   2011   2010007856
[Fic]—dc22   CIP
                                                AC

Typography by Sasha Illingworth
11 12 13 14 15   LP/RRDB   10 9 8 7 6 5 4 3 2 1
❖
First Edition

To Lisa, who taught us all how to make dragons,
and to Darrell Lum for his marvelous story
"J'Like Ten Thousand."
And special thanks to the manager and staff
of the Fairmont Copley Plaza hotel,
who made us feel so welcome on a snowy night.
And we will especially treasure
getting to know Mike.

PREFACE

I wrote this story based on my boyhood memories of Chinatown and especially of Chinese New Year's. Since firecrackers were an important part of my childhood, I couldn't leave them out.

Attitudes were different in the 1950s, and we did a lot of things as children, including buying and giving pet alligators, which I wouldn't recommend now that I'm an adult and know better.

I also want to emphasize that firecrackers were legal in San Francisco when I was a boy and that I only got to set them off when there were adults present. (I think my parents, my uncle, my aunts, and my grandparents had as much fun with them as the children did.)

Nowadays, firecrackers are illegal in most places, and, after hearing about all the injuries and fires that they can cause, I wouldn't recommend that young readers go near them, even if firecrackers are allowed in their towns and even with adult supervision.

CHAPTER ONE

September 1953

When I was a boy, Chinese people had to live in Chinatown. In those days, most landlords wouldn't sell or rent to Chinese outside of that area. Back then, there were no laws to make sellers and landlords be fair.

Mom, though, always said every cloud has a silver lining. Since my uncles, aunts, and cousins all lived in Chinatown, we got together for every holiday and birthday. Each family took turns holding a celebration.

Our parties weren't much fun for me, though. I was the youngest and the smallest. So I was never smart enough or strong enough to win any game. That was frustrating. And then my older brother, Harry, and my cousins always rubbed it in. That made me feel even worse.

The meanest cousin was Petey. He was Auntie Ellen's only child and very spoiled.

When I was eight and Petey was eleven, we had a party at his place. His flat was long but very narrow. Our large family could not gather in any single room. So Petey's parents put all their tables in the hallway one after another, making one big supertable. That's where the grown-ups ate. We kids filled up our plates there, then trooped into the living room to eat.

That was the best. We sat anywhere we wanted. On the rug. On a pillow. Even on a low bookcase. If you spilled your soda, no one scolded you. If you picked up a turkey slice with your fingers, no one got mad. If your hands were messy, no one told you to use a napkin instead of your pants.

Petey sat in a big easy chair. He looked like a tiny king on a leather throne. Everybody had to be nice to him. If you weren't, you couldn't touch his stuff. And he had the biggest collection of comics, games, and toys. As long as he was in a good mood, he would let you read or play while you snacked.

When he challenged any of us to a game of checkers, at first no one dared to accept. It was his home and his things. If he lost, he'd get mad. Then he wouldn't let us use anything anymore.

Finally, Harry offered me as a victim. Since I rarely won, Petey would stay happy.

While the others did what they wanted, I had to let Petey beat me over and over. By the sixth game, he got bored. "You're so dumb, Artie." He made a point of yawning. "What good are you?"

Petey needled me every chance he got. Before he could get going, though, the doorbell rang.

When I heard Uncle Chester's voice, that gave me an excuse to leave and go outside and greet him.

Uncle Chester was in his forties and had never married. He swept into the flat. "Artie!" he said, and gave me a big bear hug that lifted me off my feet.

When Granny asked him why he was so late, he said he'd been helping Al repair his car.

Everyone liked Uncle Chester, and Uncle Chester

liked everyone. He made everyone laugh. He made everyone happy. He was everybody's friend.

"Did you get paid?" Auntie Ellen asked.

Uncle Chester was shocked. "Of course not. He's a friend."

"That's your problem," she scolded him. "Just for once, say no when someone asks for help."

Uncle Chester shrugged. "Friends help friends."

Granny poked Auntie Ellen with her cane. "Don't pick on your baby brother."

"You spoiled him when we were kids," Dad complained. "And you're spoiling him now."

Granny jabbed Dad. "And don't pick on me, either."

Mom was safely out of reach of Granny's cane, so she took a turn at Uncle Chester as a target. "Don't you want to settle down?" she asked. "There are plenty of women who would love to have you."

Uncle Chester spread out his arms. "But they'd have to share me with the horses."

"You have horses?" I asked excitedly.

"I love to watch them," Uncle Chester explained.

"Can I watch them with you?" I asked.

"No," Mom said firmly. "Children are not allowed at the racetrack." She gave me a gentle push toward the living room. "Now go play with your cousins."

"I'd rather stay," I said. No one would tease me here.

"We're going to talk about grown-up things with Uncle," Mom said. "So scoot."

I hated to leave, but I had no choice.

Back in the living room, Petey started on me right away. "Back for more punishment, shrimp? Checkers is a baby's game anyway. Let's play Monopoly."

No one could beat Petey at that game. Uncle Steve, his dad, was a real estate agent. Petey and he practiced at Monopoly several times a week.

When no one volunteered, Petey told Harry and Dora, another cousin, to join us.

"I'm tired of games," I said. I wanted to take a turn reading comics.

But Petey insisted. "It won't be fun without you," he said. He meant he wanted to pester me some more.

"Can I play too?" Uncle Chester asked from the

doorway. He had a plate of food in his hand.

"You belong out there with the grown-ups," Dora said.

"But I'm more comfortable here," he said, sitting down by the game board. "All the 'grown-ups' want to do is pick on me." He imitated them. "'When are you going to get a real job, Chester?' 'When are you going to get married, Chester?'"

"When are you, Uncle?" Petey asked.

Uncle tapped him affectionately on the head. "Don't act so grown up."

Everyone else thought it was safe to let him stay. Since Uncle was like a big kid himself, Uncle wouldn't tell on us.

We gave him his Monopoly money. Uncle kissed it for luck and then we started playing.

The dice loved Petey. He landed on the good spaces. He bought up all the fancy deeds. Soon he had houses and hotels all around the board.

On the other hand, the dice hated me. I kept winding up on Petey's property. Soon I had no money to pay him rent. And I ran out of deeds to trade.

I should have just dropped out. Then I could

have read Petey's stack of comics. But Petey kept calling me a quitter.

That made me mad. So I asked Harry if he'd loan me some money. He refused because he didn't have a lot himself.

"Here," Uncle Chester said, and held out some Monopoly bills.

"Artie, you're such a mooch." Petey smirked.

All too soon, I landed at another one of Petey's hotels.

Petey wiggled his fingers at me. "Gimme."

"Uncle . . . ?" I asked.

"Geez, get a job, Artie," Petey said. "Quit leaning on Uncle."

"I'm not going to let family sleep out on the street," Uncle joked.

Petey's hotels were like a magnet for my token. It kept going to them. And I kept borrowing from Uncle over and over. And then Petey would make fun of me. It got worse and worse.

I felt really frustrated. Tears stung my eyes. Finally I got so mad that I threw the dice too hard. They knocked over hotels and tokens.

"Now look what you've done!" Petey snapped. "What good are you? You're a mooch. And you're useless."

"Now, now," Uncle soothed. "No need to call names." Then he gave a big sigh. "In the old days, we never had time for board games at a party. We were always having too much fun setting off firecrackers."

"It's September," Dora reminded him.

Uncle winked. "That didn't stop us when we were your age. We'd set off firecrackers even for Arbor Day. My favorites were the Phoenixes." (That was a brand of firecrackers.) "They knocked my socks off."

All my cousins stopped what they were doing. Everybody had an opinion about the best firecrackers. I think that was Uncle's plan. Petey was too busy arguing with everyone else to make fun of me.

"I like Yankee Boys," I piped up. But any would do. I loved firecrackers.

"You like firecrackers too?" Uncle laughed.

"As much as you like horses," I said.

Uncle pretended to be amazed. "That much?"

Petey dismissed me with a wave of his hand. "What would you know about firecrackers, shrimp? All you do is watch with Granny."

8

"I'll show you," I said. "This year, I'll have my own firecrackers." I was so mad that I didn't stop to think. "I'll have so many I'll . . . I'll give them away."

Petey sat back and then looked around at everyone else. "You heard Artie. He's going to give firecrackers to everyone."

I started to panic. "Wait," I said.

"I knew you were making that up," Petey crowed. "So you're not only a useless mooch, but you're a liar, too."

My stomach twisted into knots. But I was still angry. "You'll see. I'll have plenty of firecrackers."

"When you're twenty?" Petey asked.

Harry nudged me. "Don't let Petey egg you on like this."

I should have listened to Harry's warning. All I could see was Petey's smirk, though. "This Chinese New Year's," I said.

I didn't know when that was. The American year was based on the sun. The Chinese year was based on the moon. They didn't match.

Chinese New Year's always sprang out at me when I didn't expect it. Just like a jack-in-the-box. It could be months away. Or it could be soon.

I just hoped that I could figure out something by then.

"Okay." Petey nodded. "You give firecrackers to everyone, Artie, and I'll eat my words."

CHAPTER TWO

When we got home, Harry scolded me. "You know Petey's a jerk. Why didn't you keep your trap shut like I do?"

I wished I had. But it was too late now. "What do I do?" I wailed.

"Don't look at me," Harry said. "I could've loaned you the cash for one pack of firecrackers. That doesn't cost much. But then you had to be the big shot and promise firecrackers for everyone. That takes a lot of dough."

I went to the calendar in the kitchen. Mom was making tea.

"When is Chinese New Year's?" I asked her. I flipped through the pages. I didn't see it in there. I was disappointed.

"You won't find it in an American calendar," Mom explained.

She checked a small Chinese calendar that Granny had given her. "It's February third." She added, "It'll be the Year of the Horse."

Things got worse when we went to school. Petey told everyone about my boast. If I didn't give firecrackers to my family, all my friends would know. I'd never live it down.

I tried to do jobs at home to make money. I only earned a dime each time, though. I didn't think my parents would have enough work for me before Chinese New Year's. I got more and more desperate.

The next Saturday, Uncle was supposed to have lunch with us. But he didn't show up. That didn't surprise anyone. Uncle Chester always lost track of time. That's why he couldn't keep a job for long.

Uncle Chester knew that. "You carry it for us," he said to me.

Uncle Chester and I left Chinatown. We walked up Nob Hill. The streets were very steep. So we took our time.

"Is Petey giving you a hard time?" Uncle asked as we climbed along the sidewalk.

"He always does," I admitted.

"You know, I'm the youngest of my generation just like you," Uncle Chester said. "When I was your age, the family was always teasing me. They said I was useless—just like Petey said to you."

So Uncle and I were the same!

"I bet you got even when you got bigger," I said hopefully.

"Naw," Uncle Chester said. He stuck his hands in his pockets. "Because they got bigger, too. But I did show them that I could be useful. I showed everyone in Chinatown."

"Is that why you help people so much?" I asked.

Uncle Chester traced a circle above his head. "See my halo? I'm a regular saint."

"Is that why you like horses, too?" I asked.

"Sure," Uncle agreed. "Saints were kind to dumb

animals. So I figure my dough feeds all those poor little horsies, see?"

The higher we walked, the fancier the apartment houses got. Through the glass front doors, I even saw chandeliers in the lobby.

We waited at Powell Street for the cable car to go by. The conductor rang the bell and waved at Uncle Chester.

Uncle Chester waved back. "Poker next Friday, Ben?" he shouted.

"Don't bring any food!" Ben shouted back. "Just money!"

The next block was steeper. Cars went by slowly. Their engines made a lot of noise driving up. The hill was hard even on them.

Uncle Chester marched steadily up the hill. He smiled as he walked.

"Why do you look so happy?" I asked. "Aren't you tired? Aren't you worried?"

"I'm happy," he said, spreading his arms, "because I'm still alive. I learned that in the army. That's when I stopped taking things seriously. I just take it one day at a time now."

Uncle Chester had fought in World War II. He'd been in Alaska. The Japanese had taken some of the islands off the coast and he had helped take them back. But the family said he'd never been the same after he came home.

Uncle never talked about the war. Once I had to do a school report on Alaska. Since Uncle had been there, I'd tried to ask him about it.

"I don't want to talk about it," he'd said quietly. It had scared me to see him so sad. I never bothered him about it again.

Finally, we reached the top of Nob Hill. Fancy hotels and more apartment houses surrounded a little park. "Let's retrace my steps." Uncle Chester yawned again. He crossed the street to the park. "We'll start there."

His steps slowed. Maybe the long search was finally getting to him.

I wanted to find the dog. That way Uncle Chester could go home.

Uncle Chester started to whistle. "Here, Queeny. Here, girl."

There was a sort of sweet odor in the air. It made

my nose itch. "What's that funny smell?" I asked.

Uncle Chester laughed. "That's the scent of fresh-cut grass. The gardeners must have mowed the lawn."

"Oh," I said. The only lawn I knew was a small patch in the Chinatown housing projects. When I visited my friends there, we played on it. So not much grass got to grow there.

"I'll take you to Golden Gate Park sometime," Uncle Chester promised. "They've got lots of lawns there, and you can ride the merry-go-round."

A gardener stood in overalls. He was raking up the grass.

"Hey, Lennie. Any sign of a stray dog?" Uncle Chester asked.

Lennie shook his head. "I haven't seen any dogs. Just their souvenirs." He went back to raking.

Uncle Chester kept whistling and calling. I tried to whistle but I couldn't. All I could do was urge the dog in a loud voice to come to me.

Suddenly, something rustled in the hedge. The leaves grew too close together. I couldn't see inside. When I got on my knees, I couldn't see anything under the hedge, either.

But I heard a whimper.

I felt a lump in my pocket. It was Granny's beef jerky. I really liked it. But I wanted to help Uncle Chester. So I took a dark red piece from the package. The missing dog ought to be pretty hungry by now.

I waved it close to the hedge. "Here, Queeny."

A small, furry muzzle stuck out from the leaves. Her jaws opened. I yanked back the jerky. The dog's teeth snapped at the air.

I crept backward on my knees. "Come on, Queeny."

Finally, something crept out from the hedge. She was covered in mud and old leaves. She looked more like a dirty mop than a dog.

"That can't be Queeny," I said.

"Well, she sort of fits the description," Uncle said, so I tore off a strip of jerky and threw it on the ground. As the dog ate greedily, Uncle Chester studied her from all angles.

"That's her," Uncle Chester said. He started to scoop up the dog.

With a growl, the dog started to back into the hedge.

"Here, use this," I said to Uncle Chester, handing him more of the jerky.

Uncle Chester took it. The dog approached him cautiously. He tore the jerky into strips. He fed each of them to the dog. All the time, he smiled and talked to her gently. "Poor little gal. I bet you've been pretty scared."

When the strips were gone, the dog approached Uncle Chester. She sniffed at his shoes. Then she looked up hopefully.

Uncle Chester held out his hand. "Got any more?"

The dog might have been small but she was mostly stomach. I was going to have to make the ultimate sacrifice. "I was saving it for us," I complained. But I gave the last piece to Uncle Chester.

Sadly, I watched Uncle Chester feed all of it to the dog. Queeny liked the black edges of the jerky. Those were the sweetest. When the jerky was all gone, the dog whined. When Uncle reached down, Queeny licked his fingers. They must have tasted of jerky.

Uncle Chester scooped her up in his arms. "You're going home, Queeny. And then so are we."

We marched across the street to the biggest hotel. The doorman wore a big red coat with large brass buttons. On his head was a cap. He wrinkled his nose when he smelled Queeny. "You can't bring that thing in here."

"I'm Ah Choy's friend," Uncle Chester said. "And this is the missing pooch."

The doorman held out his gloved hands. "I'll take it."

"No dice," Uncle Chester said, holding Queeny close. "This dog is strictly cash on delivery."

The doorman went to a phone outside. He spoke into it. Then he jerked a thumb at the big front doors. "The manager says it's okay. Go to the front desk."

The carpet inside was so thick, my shoes sank into it. Overhead was a huge chandelier. The crystals gleamed in the light. It made all other chandeliers in the city seem like babies.

Uncle Chester marched through the lobby like he had lived here all his life. He went straight to the marble counter. He held the dog up in triumph. "I found that missing mutt."

The clerk at the counter dialed a telephone. Then he told us to wait. In a few minutes, a lady came out of an elevator. She looked familiar. Later, Uncle told me she was in the movies.

The lady spread her arms out wide. "Queeny!"

The dog leaped out of Uncle's arms. She raced past the guests and staff heading straight to the lady.

As soon as she had the dog, she began kissing it— even though it smelled a little and was pretty dirty. "I don't know how to thank you," she said to Uncle Chester.

"Friends help friends." Uncle Chester grinned.

A week later, Uncle Chester dropped by our place. He winked at me. "Ask me the time, Artie?"

I could see the clock on the mantle. "It's one o'clock."

Uncle nudged me. "Oh, go on, ask me the time."

I was puzzled but I did.

He pulled back his sleeve to reveal a fancy gold watch. "My new timepiece tells me it's six o'clock."

Dad gave a whistle. "Did you rob a bank?"

Uncle held up his forearm as he admired his watch. "I got a call from Ah Choy to come back to the hotel. The dog's owner gave it to me. Nobody's going to call me a bum when they see this."

Granny squinted at it. "It looks expensive."

Uncle tugged his sleeve back over it. "Some guy already offered me a lot of money for it. I told him no dice. I wouldn't sell it for a million bucks."

"That's right," Granny said firmly. "It's part of your luck."

"Yeah, I guess. But even if it wasn't, I wouldn't part with it," Uncle said, tapping his watch. "This is the first reward I ever got. I never had anything to be proud of before."

"You fought in the war," Dad pointed out.

"I didn't win any medals, though." Uncle shrugged.

Mom patted his arm. "You came back alive. That's what's more important."

Dad spread his hands. "Anyway, you earned this reward."

Uncle Chester winked at me. "So did your son." Then he squatted by me and whispered, "I can't give you part of the watch, but I'll help you keep your promise to Petey."

Suddenly, I felt all my worries leave me. "You will?"

He nodded. "He's got the wrong attitude. He feels big by making other people feel small." He straightened up. "And in the meantime, I'd like to give you a little bonus. Help me do your granny's shopping tomorrow."

I said okay even though I really didn't want to. I was just so happy to be off the hook.

CHAPTER THREE

U ncle Chester picked me up the next day, Sunday.
He had a list from Granny. Besides some regular stuff like soap and incense sticks, she needed
groceries. She was going to cook a meal for us.

"Bring Artie back before six," Mom told Uncle
Chester.

"We're only getting some stuff," I said.

"There's no such thing as a short walk with Uncle
Chester," Mom warned.

Uncle Chester proudly held up his watch. "How
can I be late when I've got this fine new timepiece?"

As we walked down the hill to Stockton Street, Uncle said, "Now, when I do this, Artie"—he pressed the tips of his thumb and index finger together—"you ask me the time."

Our first stop was at the Happy Paradise, a store that sold fresh fruit and vegetables in big bins and baskets. Old men and women were elbowing one another, searching the bins for the best ones. The owner was watching them like a hawk. "No pinching, no pinching," he called out to a customer.

"Hey, Sam!" Uncle Chester called.

Sam grinned when he saw Uncle Chester. Everyone did.

"Chester!" he said.

They chatted for a little while. Then Uncle introduced me.

Sam wrinkled his forehead as he studied me. "No, you're not the squash type. Hmm, and not broccoli, either. And definitely *not* kumquats."

I shifted from one foot to the other uncomfortably. "What's a kumquat?"

"A fruit that's too small for you." Sam rubbed his chin. Then he snapped his fingers. "Ah, I got it."

26

songbird and his apprentice," he said.

Uncle Chester took out Granny's list. "Mama wants a pound of your best chicken legs."

"You got it," Ah Wing said. He removed the chicken legs from a pan behind the counter. When Uncle had given him his money, Ah Wing told us to wait. Ah Wing washed his hands. Then he cut off a piece of barbecued pork and gave it to me. "This is still hot from the oven. It's payment for the concert."

It was an end piece with a blackened tip. That always tasted the sweetest.

I was so busy nibbling that I almost missed Uncle's signal. Luckily, I caught it from the corner of my eye. asked my question.

When Uncle checked his watch, Ah Wing was impressed by it.

Whenever Uncle met anyone he knew during our walk, he took off his hat. I started taking off my cap, Uncle Chester had a lot of friends, so we did that often.

Uncle gave the sign a lot, too. Almost everyone on Grant Avenue wound up learning the time and checking his watch.

He headed over to a bin.

Uncle Chester whispered to me. "Watch the technique of a pro."

Sam held his bent arms up against his sides. That way his elbows covered his ribs. Turning sideways, he slipped into a gap like a star halfback. He came back with his prize over his head. His hair was mussed up. His shirt was twisted.

"You," he said to me, "look like an orange type." He lowered his hand to show me an orange the size of a grapefruit.

"Thank you," I said, cradling it in my palms.

"Shopping here is not for amateurs." Uncle Chester laughed.

Sam straightened out his clothes. "Only sissies go to a supermarket." He wagged an index finger at me. "But there, the fruit's always spoiled and the vegetables rotten." He waved a hand at the crowded bins. "I've got nothing but the freshest and the sweetest produce. That's why everyone comes to the Happy Paradise."

Uncle gave me the signal and I asked him what the time was.

Sam's eyes got real big when he saw the watch. Naturally, he asked where Uncle had gotten it from. Naturally, Uncle told him the story.

Suddenly, a woman threw a grape on the floor and stomped on it.

"Hey," Sam said, "stop that."

She peered at the squashed grape. "I've got to see if it's fresh."

"I'd like to talk more, but duty calls," Sam said. And he headed over to argue with her.

"Is it okay if we give the orange to Granny?" Uncle Chester asked. When I nodded, he checked off an item on Granny's list. "Thanks. That's one down."

"Granny only likes sweet oranges," I said.

"If Sam picked it out for you, it's the sweetest one in the bin," Uncle Chester said. "The man may be lousy at cards, but he knows his fruit."

As we continued down the hill toward Grant Avenue, Uncle Chester began to whistle. I recognized it as the latest tune on the radio.

"How do you whistle?" I asked. I tried but I only made rude noises with my tongue.

"There's an art to whistling," Uncle Chester said. He tapped the side of his head. "And it begins up

here. It's the attitude, you see."

He tipped his hat forward. The touched his eyebrows. Then he stuck hi pockets.

"And it's the walk." He started rooster.

So I shoved my baseball cap fo copy him.

He nodded. "Now you're gettir

He puckered his lips and showed

I just made a spluttering nois

His fingers adjusted my lips.

I was still trying when we Avenue. A tourist thought I w and glared.

Uncle immediately defen sonal. He's just a budding m

After that, I was shy whistle, but Uncle urged insisted, and started to best to imitate him as w

Ah Wing stood in shop. He wore a paper h He held a hand up be

We turned up Washington Street next. On the outside of the wall of a souvenir store was a wooden stall. Ah Woo sat on a stool. He wore an old blue suit with a patch on one elbow.

"The papers just came in," Ah Woo said. He pointed to the Chinese newspapers on the rack. Uncle Chester selected the ones on Granny's list.

By now I knew to watch for the signal. When I saw it, I asked Uncle my question. Ah Woo said Uncle's watch was very nice. "But a minute on that fancy piece is the same as on one of mine." He pointed to a row of cheap watches just above his head.

I looked at the other shelves. Plastic back scratchers fanned out from a vase like the petals of a rainbow flower. Beyond them were jars of different Chinese candies. Higher on the shelves were the toys. There were wooden puzzles and popguns that shot off corks. There were papier-mâché snakes with sections that wiggled when they moved. On the highest shelves were piles of toys made out of tin. No kid could reach them up there.

Before we left, Ah Woo gave me some candied plums.

Wherever we shopped, the owners gave me little

presents. They knew if they pleased me, they would please Uncle Chester. And they liked seeing him smile. In between stores, we bumped into more of Uncle Chester's friends. Uncle made sure that all of them learned the right time.

It was late afternoon when we returned to Stockton. My pockets were stuffed with goodies. My stomach was full with snacks. But my feet were sore.

I looked at Uncle's watch. "It's five thirty," I said. "We're supposed to be home by six."

Uncle Chester checked his list. "We just have to get a jar of Lion Salve."

That was a salve for all kinds of aches and pains.

"That place has it," I said, pointing at a shop.

Uncle Chester scratched the back of his head. "Well, they don't carry the best Lion Salve."

All the jars looked the same to me. "Lion Salve's Lion Salve," I insisted.

"That's what you think," Uncle Chester said.

Then, lifting his head and putting a big smile on his face, he marched into Mimi's instead.

I was surprised, because I'd never seen Lion Salve there. But maybe I hadn't noticed it in all the clutter. Mimi had everything from T-shirts and balsa wood model kits to postcards and dishes. She also sold comic books, but if my friends and I tried to read them, Mimi always chased us away. "If you want free reading, go to the library," she would say.

Today, though, she wore a grin as large as Uncle's. When he asked for a jar of Lion Salve, she took it from beneath the counter.

Uncle didn't seem to be in any hurry, even though it was getting late. When he introduced me, Mimi pretended to scold me. "Why didn't you tell me you were Chester's nephew?"

She'd never asked. And anyway, she'd been too busy chasing us out to hold a conversation with me.

Uncle's hand gave me the sign so I asked about the time. Mimi oohed and aahed when she saw the watch. Then Uncle told her the story, including my part in it. When he was done, Uncle waved his hand toward the rack. "Go on and pick out a comic," he said.

I hesitated, glancing at Mimi.

"It's okay." She nodded.

I felt like a prince in his treasure vault as I gazed at the brightly colored covers. She'd never told that to any of us before. It was hard to know where to start.

As Uncle chatted with Mimi, I caught up on the adventures of one superhero after another. I lost track of time.

All too soon, Uncle was leaning over me. "We've got to go, sport."

"Already?" I protested.

"Which comic do you want?" Uncle asked.

I looked at the stack and managed to select three. But then I couldn't make up my mind which was the best.

So Uncle picked up all three. "Well, it's still not the same as a watch, but I'll get you all of these," he said. Uncle was always doing things like this for people.

Mimi let him pay for the Lion Salve but she tried to give the comics to me. For some reason, though, she was the one person he insisted on paying.

When we stepped outside again, the streetlights had come on. Neon signs flickered above the stores. Uncle glanced at his watch and groaned. "Man, oh man, am I in trouble. How could you let us stay there so long?"

He looked around desperately and then gave a yell. "Henry, don't close!" He raced over to a florist shop.

Henry was just starting to lock the door. But

he opened it for Uncle Chester. "What did you do now, Chester?"

"The last time I told you, it was all over Chinatown," Uncle Chester teased. He pointed to some red chrysanthemums. "I'll take those." He opened his wallet and took out two dollars. "This is all I got. Be a pal."

Henry sighed. "Okay, since it's for you."

When Henry went to wrap them, I tugged at Uncle's sleeve. "What about the firecrackers?" I asked, feeling frustrated.

Uncle slapped his forehead. "Oh yeah, your bonus. I'm real sorry, Artie. I'll make it up to you. Tell you what. I'll take you to Golden Gate Park."

I would rather have had the firecrackers, but I could never stay mad at Uncle. No one could. "Okay."

Then, loaded down with bags, we walked back up the hill to my home. At the door to our flat, he handed me the flowers. "You go in first. I'll wait outside in case your mom's mad."

When I opened the door, my nose caught all the delicious smells from the dinner table. From the clinking and clacking sounds, I knew the family was already eating.

"Mom?" I called cautiously. "I'm home."

Mom came out of the dining room. In her hand was a napkin. "Where's your uncle?" she demanded.

Desperately, I thrust the flowers out at her. "He bought you these."

"That man." Mom sighed in exasperation. She sniffed them and said in a loud voice, "Stop hiding, Chester, and come in."

Uncle Chester took a long sliding step so he stood in front of the open doorway. He held up the bags. "I've bought the stuff for dinner."

"We gave up a half hour ago and ate leftovers," Mom explained.

Granny shouted from the dining room, "I could've starved waiting for you two!" And then she laughed along with everyone else.

"Well, I hope you left some for two starving men." Tilting back his hat, Uncle whistled as he strolled inside.

That night, I thought about the day I'd spent with Uncle Chester and all his friends. Uncle Chester was someone special in Chinatown. When I was with him, I was special too.

He headed over to a bin.

Uncle Chester whispered to me. "Watch the technique of a pro."

Sam held his bent arms up against his sides. That way his elbows covered his ribs. Turning sideways, he slipped into a gap like a star halfback. He came back with his prize over his head. His hair was mussed up. His shirt was twisted.

"You," he said to me, "look like an orange type." He lowered his hand to show me an orange the size of a grapefruit.

"Thank you," I said, cradling it in my palms.

"Shopping here is not for amateurs." Uncle Chester laughed.

Sam straightened out his clothes. "Only sissies go to a supermarket." He wagged an index finger at me. "But there, the fruit's always spoiled and the vegetables rotten." He waved a hand at the crowded bins. "I've got nothing but the freshest and the sweetest produce. That's why everyone comes to the Happy Paradise."

Uncle gave me the signal and I asked him what the time was.

Sam's eyes got real big when he saw the watch. Naturally, he asked where Uncle had gotten it from. Naturally, Uncle told him the story.

Suddenly, a woman threw a grape on the floor and stomped on it.

"Hey," Sam said, "stop that."

She peered at the squashed grape. "I've got to see if it's fresh."

"I'd like to talk more, but duty calls," Sam said. And he headed over to argue with her.

"Is it okay if we give the orange to Granny?" Uncle Chester asked. When I nodded, he checked off an item on Granny's list. "Thanks. That's one down."

"Granny only likes sweet oranges," I said.

"If Sam picked it out for you, it's the sweetest one in the bin," Uncle Chester said. "The man may be lousy at cards, but he knows his fruit."

As we continued down the hill toward Grant Avenue, Uncle Chester began to whistle. I recognized it as the latest tune on the radio.

"How do you whistle?" I asked. I tried but I only made rude noises with my tongue.

"There's an art to whistling," Uncle Chester said. He tapped the side of his head. "And it begins up here. It's the attitude, you see."

He tipped his hat forward. The brim almost touched his eyebrows. Then he stuck his hands in his pockets.

"And it's the walk." He started to strut like a rooster.

So I shoved my baseball cap forward, trying to copy him.

He nodded. "Now you're getting it."

He puckered his lips and showed me how to whistle.

I just made a spluttering noise.

His fingers adjusted my lips. "Keep working at it."

I was still trying when we turned onto Grant Avenue. A tourist thought I was making rude noises and glared.

Uncle immediately defended me. "Nothing personal. He's just a budding musician."

After that, I was shy about working on my whistle, but Uncle urged me. "Never give up," he insisted, and started to whistle again. I tried my best to imitate him as we walked on.

Ah Wing stood in the doorway of his butcher shop. He wore a paper hat that looked like a little box. He held a hand up behind his ear. "Ah, here's the songbird and his apprentice," he said.

Uncle Chester took out Granny's list. "Mama wants a pound of your best chicken legs."

"You got it," Ah Wing said. He removed the chicken legs from a pan behind the counter. When Uncle had given him his money, Ah Wing told us to wait. Ah Wing washed his hands. Then he cut off a piece of barbecued pork and gave it to me. "This is still hot from the oven. It's payment for the concert."

It was an end piece with a blackened tip. That always tasted the sweetest.

I was so busy nibbling that I almost missed Uncle's signal. Luckily, I caught it from the corner of my eye. I asked my question.

When Uncle checked his watch, Ah Wing was impressed by it.

Whenever Uncle met anyone he knew during our walk, he took off his hat. I started taking off my cap, too. Uncle Chester had a lot of friends, so we did that a lot.

Uncle gave the sign a lot, too. Almost everyone on Grant Avenue wound up learning the time and admiring his watch.

We turned up Washington Street next. On the outside of the wall of a souvenir store was a wooden stall. Ah Woo sat on a stool. He wore an old blue suit with a patch on one elbow.

"The papers just came in," Ah Woo said. He pointed to the Chinese newspapers on the rack. Uncle Chester selected the ones on Granny's list.

By now I knew to watch for the signal. When I saw it, I asked Uncle my question. Ah Woo said Uncle's watch was very nice. "But a minute on that fancy piece is the same as on one of mine." He pointed to a row of cheap watches just above his head.

I looked at the other shelves. Plastic back scratchers fanned out from a vase like the petals of a rainbow flower. Beyond them were jars of different Chinese candies. Higher on the shelves were the toys. There were wooden puzzles and popguns that shot off corks. There were papier-mâché snakes with sections that wiggled when they moved. On the highest shelves were piles of toys made out of tin. No kid could reach them up there.

Before we left, Ah Woo gave me some candied plums.

Wherever we shopped, the owners gave me little

presents. They knew if they pleased me, they would please Uncle Chester. And they liked seeing him smile. In between stores, we bumped into more of Uncle Chester's friends. Uncle made sure that all of them learned the right time.

It was late afternoon when we returned to Stockton. My pockets were stuffed with goodies. My stomach was full with snacks. But my feet were sore.

I looked at Uncle's watch. "It's five thirty," I said. "We're supposed to be home by six."

Uncle Chester checked his list. "We just have to get a jar of Lion Salve."

That was a salve for all kinds of aches and pains.

"That place has it," I said, pointing at a shop.

Uncle Chester scratched the back of his head. "Well, they don't carry the best Lion Salve."

All the jars looked the same to me. "Lion Salve's Lion Salve," I insisted.

"That's what you think," Uncle Chester said.

Then, lifting his head and putting a big smile on his face, he marched into Mimi's instead.

I was surprised, because I'd never seen Lion Salve there. But maybe I hadn't noticed it in all the clutter. Mimi had everything from T-shirts and balsa wood model kits to postcards and dishes. She also sold comic books, but if my friends and I tried to read them, Mimi always chased us away. "If you want free reading, go to the library," she would say.

Today, though, she wore a grin as large as Uncle's. When he asked for a jar of Lion Salve, she took it from beneath the counter.

Uncle didn't seem to be in any hurry, even though it was getting late. When he introduced me, Mimi pretended to scold me. "Why didn't you tell me you were Chester's nephew?"

She'd never asked. And anyway, she'd been too busy chasing us out to hold a conversation with me.

Uncle's hand gave me the sign so I asked about the time. Mimi oohed and aahed when she saw the watch. Then Uncle told her the story, including my part in it. When he was done, Uncle waved his hand toward the rack. "Go on and pick out a comic," he said.

I hesitated, glancing at Mimi.

"It's okay." She nodded.

I felt like a prince in his treasure vault as I gazed at the brightly colored covers. She'd never told that to any of us before. It was hard to know where to start.

As Uncle chatted with Mimi, I caught up on the adventures of one superhero after another. I lost track of time.

All too soon, Uncle was leaning over me. "We've got to go, sport."

"Already?" I protested.

"Which comic do you want?" Uncle asked.

I looked at the stack and managed to select three. But then I couldn't make up my mind which was the best.

So Uncle picked up all three. "Well, it's still not the same as a watch, but I'll get you all of these," he said. Uncle was always doing things like this for people.

Mimi let him pay for the Lion Salve but she tried to give the comics to me. For some reason, though, she was the one person he insisted on paying.

When we stepped outside again, the streetlights had come on. Neon signs flickered above the stores. Uncle glanced at his watch and groaned. "Man, oh man, am I in trouble. How could you let us stay there so long?"

He looked around desperately and then gave a yell. "Henry, don't close!" He raced over to a florist shop.

Henry was just starting to lock the door. But

he opened it for Uncle Chester. "What did you do now, Chester?"

"The last time I told you, it was all over Chinatown," Uncle Chester teased. He pointed to some red chrysanthemums. "I'll take those." He opened his wallet and took out two dollars. "This is all I got. Be a pal."

Henry sighed. "Okay, since it's for you."

When Henry went to wrap them, I tugged at Uncle's sleeve. "What about the firecrackers?" I asked, feeling frustrated.

Uncle slapped his forehead. "Oh yeah, your bonus. I'm real sorry, Artie. I'll make it up to you. Tell you what. I'll take you to Golden Gate Park."

I would rather have had the firecrackers, but I could never stay mad at Uncle. No one could. "Okay."

Then, loaded down with bags, we walked back up the hill to my home. At the door to our flat, he handed me the flowers. "You go in first. I'll wait outside in case your mom's mad."

When I opened the door, my nose caught all the delicious smells from the dinner table. From the clinking and clacking sounds, I knew the family was already eating.

"Mom?" I called cautiously. "I'm home."

Mom came out of the dining room. In her hand was a napkin. "Where's your uncle?" she demanded.

Desperately, I thrust the flowers out at her. "He bought you these."

"That man." Mom sighed in exasperation. She sniffed them and said in a loud voice, "Stop hiding, Chester, and come in."

Uncle Chester took a long sliding step so he stood in front of the open doorway. He held up the bags. "I've bought the stuff for dinner."

"We gave up a half hour ago and ate leftovers," Mom explained.

Granny shouted from the dining room, "I could've starved waiting for you two!" And then she laughed along with everyone else.

"Well, I hope you left some for two starving men." Tilting back his hat, Uncle whistled as he strolled inside.

That night, I thought about the day I'd spent with Uncle Chester and all his friends. Uncle Chester was someone special in Chinatown. When I was with him, I was special too.

CHAPTER FOUR

When Uncle Chester asked my parents, they said I could go to Golden Gate Park. Granny was pretty upset at the suggestion. She'd heard there were wild dogs in the bushes. She was sure we'd get eaten alive.

"Artie thinks Nature is a little patch of grass in the projects," Uncle Chester argued. "He needs to see more of the world."

Granny shook her head stubbornly. "You were a great big soldier. You can take care of yourself. But Artie's too young."

"Aw, Mama," Uncle Chester coaxed, "there aren't any dogs. And if there were, they'd go for a bigger, juicier, slower target—like me."

I wanted to go. "I can run real fast, Granny."

In the end, we convinced her. "But"—Granny wagged her index finger at me—"if you hear a dog bark, you leave right away."

"We promise," Uncle Chester said. Behind his back, he had crossed his fingers.

I was really excited. The next Saturday morning, Uncle Chester picked me up right on time. But Mimi was with him too. Why was she here?

Instead of heading to the buses on Stockton, we went in the other direction to Powell. I was annoyed. The cable cars didn't run as often as the bus. The trip would take longer.

Uncle Chester paid for everybody, even for Mimi. I didn't think that was very fair. After all, she owned a whole store. How was Uncle going to get the fire-crackers if he treated her, too?

The conductor on the cable car was Ben. When the car halted at the next stop, he let me ring the bell. That made me feel special again. But then he let Mimi ring it. I didn't feel as special anymore.

Even though she horned in on our outing, I enjoyed going to the park. Except for the petting zoo. The animals smelled and the goat nearly bit my fingers.

Then we went to the aquarium in the Academy of Sciences. The halls were dark, which made the lighted tanks seem even brighter. The electric eel glared at me with its beady little eyes. And Butterball the manatee ate her cabbage by holding it against the glass and eating with a sideways motion of her mouth.

We finished at the planetarium. The dome inside blazed with stars. In Chinatown, the lights were too bright to see the stars. I hadn't realized there were so many. I didn't want to leave when the show was done.

Uncle gently pried me up from my seat. "Come on, Artie. We've got to get home before your granny calls the cops because the wild dogs are chasing you."

"Or the goats." I chuckled. I finally got up.

Uncle shook his head as we left the room. "Boy, aren't those stars something? If I could make one of those, I'd put it up in the sky so it could make every-one happy."

He was still raving about them on the way home. And Mimi kept nodding.

Afterward, when Uncle dropped me off, I com-plained to Mom about Mimi.

Mom just laughed. "Uncle's lonely."

That seemed silly to me. "He's got us," I protested.

"He's lonely in a different way," Mom explained. "When you're older, you'll understand. In the mean-time, be nice to her."

Another weekend, the three of us visited the zoo. Uncle imitated the monkeys so well that some kids threw him peanuts. Later, he gathered them up and we fed them to the elephants.

The weekend I enjoyed the most was the ferry ride. I liked going under the deck and watching the big pistons go up and down. Then we went back on deck. Mimi fed some popcorn to a seagull. All his cousins joined him. They demanded their share with loud squawks. Their beaks opened wide.

"They remind me of my cousins," Mimi laughed

as she threw out another handful.

I wished she hadn't said that. It made me think of my cousins. Only they'd want firecrackers, not popcorn.

Even though Mimi gave the seagulls all her popcorn, they still wanted more.

Uncle put one arm around Mimi. He slid the other around me. "Inside," he said.

We ran into the big cabin on the deck. Then Uncle slid the door shut. Outside, the flock flew around squawking.

"They left a souvenir," Mimi said. She handed him a handkerchief. Then she pointed at the white spot on his jacket.

It was all her fault. She shouldn't have been chuckling. But Uncle was laughing too. Maybe he was just being polite.

I tried my best to be nice to Mimi like Mom said. But Mimi was just a friend and I was family. She had no right to hog him so much for herself.

But then one Saturday we went out to Playland by Ocean Beach. Each seat in the roller coaster car could only take two people. I wanted to be with Uncle. But he started to sit with Mimi.

I couldn't help looking mad.

Mimi saw my face. "No, Chester. You should ride with Artie. He's still small."

Now she was insulting me. "I'm not little," I protested.

"Of course you're not, Artie," Mimi said soothingly. "But I'm going to be pretty frightened myself. I think your uncle would be better off with you."

"Well, I got to hold on to someone when I get scared," Uncle said.

We got in the front row. Mimi sat in back of us. As the car rose and then dipped suddenly, I felt good. I let Uncle grab my arm.

Afterward, as a reward, Uncle took us to a place that baked apple turnovers fresh. They were delicious even if they burned my mouth. But part of me wished he'd used the money for firecrackers instead.

As we passed by a shooting gallery, I saw it had lots of prizes. But the best was the hugest teddy bear I'd ever seen.

"My turn to show off," Uncle said.

He paid his money and hefted the rifle. It looked small in his hands. Closing one eye, he squinted over the sights carefully. Rows of ducks and pipes slid by.

Then he took a breath and fired.

Ping!

The bullet knocked a duck over.

Ping! Ping!

Ducks and pipes disappeared.

Uncle didn't miss. In no time, he had won the huge teddy bear.

When the man held out the bear to Uncle, I saw it was almost as big as me. I really liked it. But Uncle passed it to Mimi. He must have felt sorry for Mimi. "At least the army taught me one thing that's handy."

As soon as Mimi had it, she gave it to me. "Here, Artie."

I couldn't imagine giving away such a wonderful prize. I hugged it gratefully.

"Don't you want it?" I asked, puzzled.

"I got my teddy bear," Mimi said. And she took Uncle's arm.

Uncle laughed a lot, but never like this. It was the happiest I ever heard him. I guessed this was what Mom had meant.

I thought about the roller coaster. Maybe Mimi had tried to share Uncle at the time just like she was sharing the bear with me now.

I decided right then and there that Mimi was pretty okay. She made Uncle glad. And I liked anyone who did that. So it was time to stop being a baby. What counted was Uncle's happiness.

I wondered if Mimi liked firecrackers too. Between me and her, Uncle was bound to buy them.

When Uncle went to the restroom, I saw my chance. "Hey, Mimi. Do you like firecrackers?"

She made a face and covered up her ears. "No, they're way too noisy."

I was disappointed. I'd have to work on Uncle myself.

CHAPTER FIVE

December 1953

After that, I became used to Mimi being around. So did everyone else. She got along with everyone just fine. The family even invited her to Thanksgiving and the birthday parties.

I visited Mimi often. I could sit and read as long as I wanted. Everybody else had to buy their comics and leave right away.

My schoolmates asked me how I did it. I just told them that Mimi and I were buddies.

I liked Mimi now. But not just because of the

comics. She liked Uncle. And I liked anyone who liked him.

One day before Christmas vacation, I was in the store, reading. Even though the American school had ended, I still had Chinese school.

Mimi asked me, "Are you looking forward to Christmas?"

"Sure." I selected a comic. "Who doesn't?"

Mimi's finger traced a design on the counter. "Has Chester . . . said what he wants for Christmas?"

I wanted to say comic books. But that would be a present for me, not for him. And I had to be good. After all, Christmas was near. "Granny says he needs new socks."

Mimi folded her arms. "That's what he *needs*. But I think Chester would want something fun."

"Uncle Chester has fun with everything," I pointed out.

"True," she admitted, "but I want to get something special for a special guy."

Not everyone saw how unique Uncle was. I liked Mimi even more now.

I thought for a moment.

I said with sudden hope, "He likes firecrackers."

Mimi scrunched up her nose. "I told you. They make too much noise, and they stink."

I scratched my head. "Well, he's always playing with my toys."

She scratched the tip of her nose. "What sort of toys?"

I thought about it. "They should move and make a lot of noise."

"Like the tin ones at Ah Woo's?" Mimi asked.

I said those would be fine.

I didn't mind shopping for toys. Mimi closed up the store and we went to Ah Woo's stall. My eyes drifted up to the top shelf. I saw the packets wrapped in red paper with the colorful labels. Some had flying gorillas, and others had warriors in armor or spacemen or flying saucers.

I wished Mimi liked firecrackers as much as she liked Uncle. It couldn't be helped, though.

And then, because Mimi was there, Ah Woo got on a stool and took down the tin toys. And I forgot the firecrackers for a while. There were cars, buses, airplanes, tanks, spaceships, and almost everything else. It was hard to choose.

Mimi asked Ah Woo, "What toy moves the most

and makes the most noise?"

Ah Woo scratched his head. "They all look and sound the same to me."

So Mimi asked me to try them out.

After I had tested them all, Mimi asked me, "What do you think?"

I liked the spaceship. Its jets were red plastic and flashed when it moved along the sidewalk. I was tempted to pick it, but I told myself to think about Uncle and choose what *he* would like.

So I handed her a tank. When you wound it, its treads rolled relentlessly over everything. Sparks flew from its cannon and it made loud, grinding noises. It was perfect for Uncle.

"This one," I said.

CHAPTER SIX

Christmas 1953

A t Christmas, the whole family got together at our place. Mimi was there, too.

She could hardly wait for Uncle to open her present. Neither could I.

When he finally unwrapped it, he stared at the socks.

Granny reminded him of his manners. "What do you say?"

Uncle tried real hard to sound enthusiastic. "Oh

gee, something I needed. And they're red. My favorite color."

"Look real hard," Mimi laughed.

Underneath the socks was the toy tank.

Uncle Chester held it up in both hands. His eyes gleamed. "And something I really wanted."

It was funny, though—he didn't know what to do with it. He turned it over and over in his hands and said, "Isn't this neat?" But all he did was just look at it.

"Grown-ups," Dora said. Then we showed him how to play with it.

He sat and shook his head in wonder. "Is that how it goes?"

It was a good Christmas for me, too. I got mostly toys and hardly any clothes. It was almost perfect except for Petey. He kept bugging me about the firecrackers.

"Are you *really* going to buy me firecrackers?" he asked. "Or should I save up my money?"

I thought of Uncle's promise. "You'll get them." I glared at him.

"Hey, everyone," Petey announced to our cousins. "Artie is going to keep his promise. So don't anyone buy firecrackers for Chinese New Year's."

"Quit picking on him," Harry said. Since we were at our house, he didn't have to be nice to Petey.

Petey got all big-eyed and innocent. "Don't you believe your own little brother?"

Harry knew how empty my pockets usually were. "Aw, just leave the pip-squeak alone. It's Christmas."

I glanced at Uncle. He just winked.

I just hoped he could pull it off and give Big-Mouth Petey a big surprise.

CHAPTER SEVEN

January 27, 1954, to February 2, 1954
Last week before Chinese New Year's

The American New Year always comes before Chinese New Year. And right on January first, Uncle was the one who got a lot of surprises. All of them nasty. He bet on some horses. The nags all lost. So did the basketball teams he bet on.

Worse, the jobs dried up.

His friends were really sorry. But times were tight for them, too.

So Uncle lost his smile.

There was one benefit, though. I saw him more. He often came to our home to eat. But he didn't joke anymore. He didn't laugh, either. He just sat there like a lump.

He stopped bringing Mimi to our home, too.

I shouldn't have minded. After all, I didn't have to share Uncle anymore. But I kept remembering how happy he'd looked when she was with us. That was a good enough reason to check up on her. But she'd also given me all those comics. I owed her.

Finally, in the last week of January, I went into Mimi's store. She looked worried and sad too. She said Uncle didn't return her calls anymore. She asked me how he was.

I got real uncomfortable. "He's fine," I said.

"Are you taking care of him?" she asked. She seemed ready to cry.

I promised her that we were. Then I left.

I decided not to go there anymore. I didn't like to see Mimi so unhappy.

That night Uncle Chester came to dinner. He brought along a jar of honey, and he took that into the kitchen first.

Food was bubbling on the stove. Near it was a picture of the Kitchen God. Opening the jar, Uncle dabbed some honey on the Kitchen God's mouth.

"What are you doing?" I asked.

"The Kitchen God has to go up to Heaven and report on us," Mom explained. "So we're giving him something to eat before he makes that long trip."

Harry winked. "We're bribing him not to tell on us."

I figured I could use some help, too. So I smeared some honey on his mouth as well.

Then we took the picture down and burned it in the sink. Smoke rose up from it. It drifted through the open window like a gray snake. The sky was a small black rectangle between the buildings. The smoke rose in a thin ribbon toward it.

"Say only nice things about us," I told the Kitchen God, "especially about Uncle."

Uncle had also bought a new picture of the Kitchen God for us. He told me we'd hang the new one up during New Year's. That was when the Kitchen God was supposed to come back.

I asked him, "Why don't you put it up in your kitchen?"

"Because I never use it," Uncle Chester said. "I'm always mooching meals off someone in the family."

"You know you're always welcome here," Dad said, and Mom, my uncle, and my aunt nodded.

"You said I was useless," Uncle said. "Once a bum, always a bum."

Dad groaned. "You've got a memory like an elephant. We were kids when I said that."

Mom shoved Uncle out of the kitchen. "You'll feel better after you've eaten."

When we sat down at the dinner table, I tried to tell Uncle about Mimi.

He just got mad. "Mind your own business," he snapped.

I got mad myself. "She was crying."

"Aw, she's better off without a bum like me," Uncle said.

Under the table, Mom nudged me to be quiet.

Dad cleared his throat as he picked up his knife and fork. "I tried to call you today, Chester. But your telephone service has been cut."

Uncle shoveled some peas into his mouth. It gave him an excuse not to talk until he finished chewing.

He kept his eyes on his plate. "It's just a misunderstanding," he mumbled.

"And I know your landlady," Auntie Ellen said. "She says you didn't pay your rent. She's very upset."

"Another misunderstanding," Uncle insisted.

"Do you need some money to tide you over?" Dad asked.

Uncle grunted. "Didn't Mom teach you anything? You're supposed to pay your debts before Chinese New Year's—not wind up with a new one."

"What about the guys you made the bets with?" Uncle Steve asked. "Are you going to be able to settle up with them?"

"Where there's a will, there's a way," Uncle insisted.

It was quiet at the table after that. There was just the clanking of knives and forks on the plates.

When we were done, Harry, Petey, and I cleared the table. As we stacked the dishes in the sink, Petey asked, "Have you bought the firecrackers yet?"

Uncle was more important than my reputation. "No."

Of course, Petey began to make fun of me.

Harry tried to defend me. "Leave him alone," he said.

But Petey kept right on with it. I got so mad, I didn't know whether to cry or hit him. I felt like doing both.

"That's enough," Uncle Chester said from the doorway. He'd heard us from the dining room.

He strode into the kitchen angrily. Petey hunched his shoulders. Suddenly, he looked really small.

Uncle leaned over Petey. "Artie's a man of his word. When he makes a promise, he keeps it."

"It's all right, Uncle," I said. I was ready to take the blame.

Harry and I shared a bedroom. I had the top bunk. I couldn't get to sleep that night. I kept worrying about Uncle. As I tossed and turned, I felt a kick from below. "Lie still," Harry grumbled. "You make enough noise for an earthquake."

"Harry?" I asked.

"What?" came his sleepy reply.

"Uncle's got a lot of troubles," I said. "What do

you think he's going to do?"

"You've got problems of your own." Harry yawned. "Didn't you tell me Uncle would pay for the firecrackers?"

"Yeah," I said. Because I had been counting on Uncle, I'd spent what I'd saved. I had no money now. I couldn't even buy a pack for Petey.

He would tell everyone when I broke my promise. I could have told people that Uncle had broken his word to me. But he couldn't help it. And besides, I would never treat Uncle that way. He was more important than my own reputation.

"Harry, don't tell anyone about Uncle's promise, okay?" I asked.

"'Kay," Harry mumbled, and started to snore.

The next morning I was still pretty worried about Uncle, so I didn't even think about my own problems. When I got to school, I saw kids staring at me and whispering. I didn't know why until I got to class.

Sid sat behind me. He poked me in the back. "How come you didn't invite me?"

I turned around. "Invite you to what?"

"To the party. Petey told us you were giving out

free firecrackers," Sid said.

That darn Petey. I looked around. My other class-mates looked as eager as Sid. I had to stop the rumor now. "It's just for family."

Sid looked disappointed. "But Petey said—"

"Don't believe anything he tells you," I said.

Tap. Tap. Tap.

To my horror, I saw the ruler rapping my desk. "Don't let me interrupt you," Sister Barbara said.

Sister Barbara was the biggest nun in the school. Except for the white cardboard around her throat, she was dressed in an all-black habit. She looked like a volcano with a pink face and snow beneath her chin.

I cringed. Sister's ruler hit hands as well as desks. "I'm sorry, sister."

The volcano rested her ruler against her shoulder. It was ready to strike. "I know you're planning a big party, but your social life can wait until recess."

Even Sister had heard the gossip!

To my relief, she wheeled around. She lifted the book in her other hand and began to read the lesson out loud.

I spent the rest of the day explaining to everyone

that only my family was getting firecrackers. It disappointed a lot of people and made a few angry.

I'd just have to take it. I'd been stupid enough to boast about buying the firecrackers in the first place. It wasn't Uncle's fault he couldn't help me now.

When the last school bell rang, I just wanted to hide at home, but Petey and his friends were waiting for me in the courtyard. "Have you bought the firecrackers yet, Boom-Boom Boy?" Petey asked.

"No," I confessed.

Petey's bunch began to make fun of me.

"Leave me alone," I said, trying to climb the steps to the street.

They stayed with me and kept right on with their teasing. Boom-Boom Boy was the mildest insult. I got so mad, I didn't know whether to cry or hit someone. I felt like doing both.

"That's enough," Uncle Chester said. He was standing at the top of the stairs. He had a plastic bag in his hand.

Petey's friends edged away.

Petey turned real pale and then ran, his friends close behind him.

Uncle watched them retreat down the street. "Has

he been making trouble for you over your promise?"
Uncle asked.

"It's all right, Uncle," I said. I was ready to take
the blame.

"Where there's a will, there's a way," Uncle
reminded me again. He handed me a bag of oranges.
"Sam gave me these. Take them home to your parents as a thank-you for all the meals."

Turning on his heel, he walked away.

CHAPTER EIGHT

As I checked off the days to Chinese New Year's, I knew I would never live it down. Petey would see to that. But I didn't care about that anymore. I was more worried about Uncle Chester.

Finally, on the morning before the new Chinese year, Mom went around running her finger along the windowsills.

Her fingertips turned black in no time. "This house is filthy," she declared. "New Year's means a clean house."

She got out the buckets and mops and sponges and brooms and vacuum. Mom put Harry and me to work. Then, for a while, I was too busy to think about Uncle.

When we finished cleaning the house, Mom got out the special scrolls. They were long strips of red paper, and on them, her father had written little bits of poems in Chinese.

I had never met my grandfather. However, when we unrolled the scrolls, the paper made loud crinkling sounds. And I would imagine I was hearing my grandfather laughing from far away and long ago.

I looked at the characters written in big, broad strokes. I couldn't read all of them yet, so Mom translated them for me. They wished us health, wealth, and happiness. I just hoped some of the good wishes rubbed off on Uncle.

As Mom hung up the scrolls, I put my nose against the paper and sniffed. There was still a little perfume left in the ink. And I thought my grandfather had used that special ink on purpose. Just so his grandson could smell it years later.

We had finished hanging the scrolls when we

heard a knocking at the door. It was Uncle Chester.

His suit was clean and freshly pressed. In his arms was a potted narcissus. "This is a thank-you for all the free meals you gave me," he explained. He pointed to the buds. "It should bloom right around New Year's."

Mom stared at the plant. "Did you win the lottery?"

"Some, um, investments paid off finally," Uncle said to her. Then he ruffled my hair. "I told you that there's always a way."

"That's great," I said, feeling very relieved.

Uncle tipped his hat back. "But Chinese New Year's is more than a new year. It's a new you. You're getting shaggy. So am I. Time for a haircut."

"What will Father do?" I asked. "He's bald."

Uncle laughed. "We'll get my big brother some polish so he can make his head shine like a mirror."

Uncle Chester took me down to Waverly Place. There were a half dozen barbershops on just one block.

We went into one crowded shop. Everyone else wanted to get a haircut too.

The customers and barbers all knew Uncle.

Uncle took a roll of money from his pocket. He took off the clip and peeled off some bills. "Here's the money I owe you," he said, and handed them to the barber.

The barber put the money into his pocket. "I hope I didn't lean on you too much, Chester. No hard feelings?"

Uncle slapped him on the shoulder. "Hey, it's New Year's."

While we waited, Uncle and the other patrons studied a newspaper called the *Racing Form*.

Uncle liked Top of the Morning. The others weren't so sure.

"Who's that?" I asked Uncle.

"She's a horse," Uncle explained.

"She's an old glue pot," another man insisted.

Uncle got annoyed. "She's a fine thoroughbred. She comes from a great family," Uncle said, and patted his chest. "Just like me."

"Then you better watch it or you could wind up in the glue factory too." The barber laughed.

After the haircut, my ears felt cooler. The barber had patted sweet stuff on my head. It stung at first. When Uncle and I left, we smelled almost as good as the flowers in the park.

Then Uncle Chester and I walked toward Grant

Avenue. At the corner, he stopped and took a deep breath. "Get a whiff of that, Artie."

I sniffed the air. "All I can smell is my hair."

Uncle patted his chest. "Breathe real deep."

So I did. The scent was even stronger than the stuff the barber put on me. It was like a bin of oranges all mixed up with the flower gardens at Golden Gate Park. I rubbed my nose. "That's not Chinatown."

"That, my dear nephew, is the scent of Chinese New Year's," Uncle said.

"I never noticed it before," I said. Mom had been right. I didn't need a calendar. My nose would have told me the right day.

"That's the trouble nowadays. Everyone's in such a rush that they miss what's in front of them," Uncle said, jamming his hands into his pockets. "You got to take your time, Artie. You know, stroll."

Sprigs of plum and cherry blossoms had sprouted in big tin cans outside the stores. Whole dwarf orchards perfumed the sidewalks. Flowers clung to branches like tiny, pale butterflies.

The bins outside the stores had become miniature Egypts. Bright oranges, round as Christmas ornaments, rose in pyramids. Tangerines, with twigs and green leaves still attached, were heaped around them. Next to them squatted giant, fat pomelos, yellow as turbans, filling the air with a sharp, cough-drop scent.

Mouthwatering aromas came from the restaurants. In the window of one place was a whole roast pig with crisp skin. Stores and stalls had all sorts of candies. There were even ready-made circular trays with eight compartments for different kinds of candied fruit, nuts, and seeds. Each brought its own brand of good luck.

The smells tickled and pinched and delighted my nose. New Year's would be here soon.

And everywhere Chinatown was red, red, red. Dad said it was the color of life—like blood. He said it also symbolized the south, which is where our family had come from in China. Granny insisted it meant good luck and happiness and riches. Whatever red really meant, I figured you wanted some of it.

The stores hung up red scrolls too. None were as nicely done as Grandfather's, though.

"Chinatown looks just like the inside of a big firecracker," I said excitedly to Uncle Chester.

Uncle turned slowly, looking around. "Yeah, come to think of it, it does. I can't wait for New Year's, can you?"

I think he was even more excited than me. "Neither can I," I agreed. "But don't worry about Petey. I'll handle him."

"A promise is a promise," Uncle insisted. "I'll keep my word to you and you'll keep your word to Petey."

As always when we strolled through the crowds, Uncle met friends everywhere. Unlike my other walks with Uncle, though, some of them didn't smile at first. These were the ones to whom he owed money. However, when he paid them, they grinned broadly and said they knew they could trust him.

The last one was a man with a big cigar. When Uncle settled up with him, he asked, "Say, have you got the time, Chester?"

Uncle looked at his wrist. "It's seven o'clock."

Instead of his expensive watch, he was wearing one of Ah Woo's cheap ones.

"What happened to your watch?" I asked.

Uncle shrugged. "I got tired of it."

"But you loved that watch," I said.

The man with the cigar bent over. He stank of tobacco. "Your uncle's supposed to pay his debts before New Year's."

Suddenly, I realized what Uncle had given up. As the man left us, I stood there, horrified and ashamed. "You sold your watch," I said. I felt like crying.

Uncle moved me out of the way as a man wheeled a hand truck full of crates past us. "Look, Artie. Once I got stuck with the name of a bum, it stuck to me like glue. I was there when Petey picked on you. What happened to me is starting to happen to you. But I'm not going to let it. We're going to nip this thing in the bud."

"Forget the firecrackers. Please. Get the watch back," I begged.

Uncle squatted down so we were eye to eye. "Anyway, part of that watch was yours. So I owe you. And you know me. I settle *all* my debts before New Year's."

CHAPTER NINE

U ncle tried to cheer me up as we finished the shopping. But I was too sad to smile.

When I got home, I told Mom everything.

Mom sighed. "He shouldn't have sold his watch, but that's just like Chester. Don't feel bad, though. It wasn't just the promise he made for you. He owed money to other people. It's a point of honor to pay them back before New Year's."

I remembered what Uncle had said about being called a bum. "Did everyone pick on him when he was a kid?" I asked.

"He got teased a lot," Mom admitted. "And sometimes when you hear something often enough, you believe it. So I guess that's why he thinks he's a bum—even when he's not."

The watch had made him so proud. He hadn't felt like a bum then. And Granny had said it was part of his luck now. "Can't we get his watch back for him?" I asked.

Mom shook her head. "It was a very expensive watch. We don't have that kind of money." Granny couldn't buy it for Uncle either. She had less money than us.

"It's all my fault," I said.

"Don't be sad," Mom said gently. "Your uncle made a big sacrifice for you. It's important to accept his gift. He wants you to be happy."

I couldn't pretend to be glad. And I couldn't leave it alone, either.

So the next day I went to the one person who might help me.

Mimi was very busy. Lots of people were buying cards and *li see*, little red envelopes. They had good wishes on them for riches or long life or other good stuff. They also had pictures of dragons or flowers in gold ink or even in full color. Folks put money inside the *li see*. And the money ought to be new—either shiny coins or crisp dollar bills.

I had to wait a while until there were no customers at the cash register.

"Well, hello, stranger," Mimi said. "I thought you were avoiding me, too."

I went near the end of the counter so I could talk low. I told Mimi everything.

Mimi pressed her lips together. "Your uncle made it clear that he doesn't want me."

I stared up at her. "He still likes you."

Mimi rubbed at a spot on the countertop. "Then why doesn't he come by?"

"He thinks he's not good enough for you," I said.

"Then your uncle's being stupid," Mimi said.

"Maybe he doesn't need the watch. Maybe he just needs you," I suggested.

Mimi tapped her fingers on the counter. "Did he say that?"

"No," I said. When she frowned, I added hastily, "But he's thinking it."

Mimi sniffed. "It's none of my business now. Consider me a stranger."

She'd been my last hope. Sadly, I started to leave.

"Artie," she said.

I turned around.

She waved at the comic book rack. "Help yourself to something."

"Thank you," I said, "but I can't take gifts from strangers."

CHAPTER TEN

I felt so useless. That night, I just wanted to hide in the bedroom, but Mom and Dad made me get in our old car. It wheezed slowly up the steep hill to Cousin Dora's. Her family was holding the celebration on New Year's Eve.

On a table in the hallway was a big bowl of oranges, tangerines, and pomelos. Towers of paper plates and wax cups rose like a city next to them.

Granny was already in the kitchen. A big pot of water boiled on top of the stove. As we walked in, she picked up a chicken. The poultry shop had left on its head and feet. I tried not to look in its eyes as Granny put it into the pot. Later, the broth would make good soup.

Frying pans and woks were stacked all around. Spoons and spatulas and long wooden chopsticks lay in a row like a surgeon's tools. Big pots of rice were already cooked, dry and fluffy the way my granny liked it. Everything else was cut up and waiting for her wizardry.

As the heat and excitement increased in the kitchen, Granny shed her sweater. Then she took off her vest. She shrank in size as she cooked. Mom, my aunts, and I scurried to keep up with Granny. But that was impossible. Granny was like a small whirlwind twirling about the kitchen.

Finally, Granny allowed us to carry out the bowls of food to the dining room. There was a noodle dish called *jai* with lots of thin, transparent noodles, crunchy ginkgo nuts, chewy strips of dried bean curd, and other tasty stuff.

The chicken was also laid out along with a fish, complete with tail and head and eyeballs like small marbles. Granny had prepared a lot of other wonderful dishes as well, like sweet-and-sour shrimp.

Granny looked around at the seated family. "Where's my baby boy?" She frowned. "I told him to be on time."

"Chester's not here yet, Mama," Dad said. "Should we wait?"

"No, the food will get cold." Granny sighed. But everyone could see she didn't want to start without Uncle Chester.

Just then, the doorbell rang. It was Uncle Chester. When he saw all the food on the table, he asked, "Am I late?"

"Better get that fancy watch fixed," Uncle Steve joked.

Uncle Chester tugged his sleeve down. He wanted to make sure the cheap watch was hidden. "I guess I'll have to."

I felt even worse after that.

When we had all sat down, Granny apologized to everyone. She had very high standards for cooking. And so she found something wrong with each of her dishes. Of course, everything was delicious. The only one unhappy with the meal was my granny.

Uncle smiled and laughed a lot through dinner. But his smile was always a little too big and his laugh

76

too loud. He was trying to fool everyone. He wanted us to think he was the same as always.

Uncle caught me watching him. He misunderstood. After dinner, he whispered to me, "Don't worry, Artie. Everything's been taken care of."

I wanted to tell him to get his money back. But Mom knew what I was thinking. She shook her head. So I didn't say anything.

CHAPTER ELEVEN

February 3, 1954

First day of Chinese New Year's

The next day, we gathered again to celebrate the first day of the New Year. This time Uncle Andy hosted the party. There were trays of bright red barbecued spareribs, platters of fried drumsticks coated in Auntie Ethel's special bread crumbs, and plates of mushrooms stuffed with chopped sausage and meat. And a fun dish of ground pork, chestnuts, mushrooms, and oyster sauce that you wrapped in a lettuce leaf. It was awfully good but awfully messy.

Auntie Ethel and her two children, Cindy and Ernest, put out a lot of other delicious dishes too.

Everything had been sliced up the night before. Granny didn't like us to use knives and scissors during New Year's. She said it might cut the good luck for the New Year.

Uncle Chester made sure to come early. I thought he'd have a big bag of firecrackers with him. But his hands were empty.

Still, he had said everything would be okay. So I tried not to worry.

Uncle Andy's place had a dining room big enough to hold all of us. The adults sat at the main table in the center. The children sat at smaller tables against the wall.

As I came in, Petey made a point of sitting next to me. "So where's my firecrackers, shrimp?" he asked.

I had faith in Uncle.

"Don't worry," I said. "You'll get them."

Petey studied me from different angles. "I think your nose must be growing because that's such a whopper."

Uncle Andy scolded him. "Hey, no teasing. No insults. No fights. And no play-battles, either. We hid all of Ernie's cap guns."

"That's right. You all get along with one another," Granny added, "or the quarreling will stay with us for the rest of the year."

That didn't stop Petey. When no one but me was looking, he'd pretend to light firecrackers. Then he'd spread his fingers like they were exploding.

The trouble was that the kids finished before the adults.

While the grown-ups ate and talked about the past, all we could do was wait.

Dora got bored. She forgot and started to drum her chopsticks on her plate.

Her mother told her to stop that. You never played with your chopsticks at any time of the year. You weren't even allowed to drop them. It was bad luck, but especially at New Year's.

Dad chuckled. "Be glad Granny doesn't follow *all* the old customs. In other families, daughters-in-law like your mom would have to bow and give her a cup of tea. It's a sign that they're not the boss. But in our family, everyone already knows your granny's in charge. But when Granny believes in a custom, you'd better keep it."

Finally, Uncle Chester got up from his chair. "Come on, everyone." He led us all into the kitchen. He pointed to all the big bottles of soda. "Let's mix the different sodas. The one with the most disgusting color wins."

Everybody but me joined in. "What's the matter, Artie?" Uncle asked. "Don't you want to win?"

I couldn't tell him how sad I felt. "I . . . I just don't feel like it," I said.

For a moment, Uncle looked even sadder than me. But then Harry and my cousins were calling to him. They wanted him to try his hand.

He put the broad grin back on his face. "All right. Watch this."

He was trying so hard to appear happy. And I realized I was only making it more difficult for him. And that wasn't right. I remembered what Mom had said. I had to accept Uncle's gift. So I had to try my best to look like I was glad, too.

I went over to the counter where all the sodas were. "Can I have a turn, too?"

Harry won with a drink brown as mud. Which he then had to gulp down. He said it tasted as disgusting as it looked.

Uncle wasn't sure what to do next. But I had an idea. "Let's have our own New Year's parade."

The real parade would take place after New Year's, when everyone in Chinatown was free.

We made one of Dora's dolls our own Miss Chinatown and put her on a wagon.

Then we joined sheets together with safety pins. That would be the dragon's body. Dora was really good at art. She used crayons to turn a big cardboard box into a dragon's head.

Uncle Chester took the head. Then Harry and my cousins got behind him under the sheets. The smaller children like me drummed on the bottoms of pots to set a rhythm for our sneakers' squeaks.

Leading with the doll float, we circled the table. The racket swelled within the apartment until we even drowned out Uncle Chester's big, booming laugh.

Uncle Andy held up his hands. "Okay, okay, we give up!"

The grown-ups began reaching into their pockets and purses for *li see*.

We politely wished them happiness and wealth: *Goong hay fat choy*. And Cindy and Ernest, who were the politest of all, simply wished them a happy New Year: *Sun Ning Fai Lok*.

For a moment, I couldn't help forgetting about Uncle's watch as the small red envelopes piled up in my hand. Uncle Fred gave us each an envelope with a picture of a carp. Then, like the schoolteacher he was, he told us how the Chinese word for carp was a pun on another Chinese word for success.

"That's not the only reason," Granny said. She told us about a certain gate in China. If a carp could make the difficult swim through it, the carp could become a dragon. And that's what any sensible fish would wish, because dragons were so powerful and magical.

We'd heard it all before, so I pretended to be paying attention. But my fingers were squeezing the envelopes to guess the size of the coins inside.

"Rich families only give out dollar bills," Petey grumbled softly.

But I was glad to get anything.

Weeks before, my mother would go through any change she got, saving the shiniest quarters. Uncle Chester always gave out large, shiny fifty-cent pieces while Uncle Fred always gave out nickels. And his *li see* were always somehow damp from his sweaty pocket so the dye came off on my fingertips.

Granny always made Uncle Chester come over. "What do you say, baby boy?"

"You don't have to do this, Mama," Uncle Chester told her.

"You're not married yet," Granny said. "And you'll always be a boy to me."

"*Goong hay fat choy,*" Uncle Chester said.

And Granny gave him his own *li see*. It was fatter than the others. I think it had a lot of money. "Now don't spend this on the horses," she told him. "Use it wisely. Like on Mimi."

Uncle held the *li see* flat on his palm. He hesitated to take it.

"Aw, Mama," Uncle Chester said.

"You listen to your mama. She's good for you," Granny insisted. She closed his fingers around the *li see*. "Or use it when you need it."

CHAPTER TWELVE

D ad slapped the side of his head when Uncle nodded at him. "Sorry, Artie. I forgot your stuff in all the excitement," he said. "I left it in the auto. I'll go get it."

I was puzzled. I hadn't brought anything.

Dad came back a moment later with a shopping bag bulging with firecrackers! I guess Uncle had given them to Dad a few days ago. I hadn't noticed it with all the other junk in our car trunk.

Petey's jaw dropped. Even Harry stared in disbelief.

Dad set the bag down and cupped his hands

around his mouth like a megaphone. "Okay. It's time for Artie's big show!"

I swallowed. It was bad enough Uncle had sacrificed his watch. I couldn't take the credit away from him. "It's Uncle's show. He bought them all, not me."

"It's Uncle Chester's and *your* show," Granny corrected me. "It's a gift from the youngest of the generations to the older ones. Right?" She looked around the family. Not even Petey dared to contradict her.

Harry elbowed Petey then. "Artie kept his promise. Now it's time to keep yours."

"Okay," Petey said in a small voice. "Artie's not a mooch."

"Or . . . ?" Harry prompted.

Petey got red in the face. "Or a liar. Or useless."

Auntie Ellen frowned. "When we get home, young man, we are going to talk about calling other people names."

I was really glad I wasn't Petey. Auntie Ellen was famous for her scolding. Even my parents didn't cross her.

All of us, grown-ups and kids, trooped outside. The moon had vanished beneath a cloud of dark purple wool. "It looks like rain," Uncle Steve grumbled.

"New Year's always brings the dragon," Granny said simply, "and the dragon always brings rain."

Uncle and I handed out the firecrackers. The adults and bigger children like Harry got larger firecrackers.

"What do you say?" his mother reminded Petey when he got his.

"Thank you, Artie," he mumbled humbly.

Younger kids got smaller firecrackers called ladyfingers, row after row of dainty little cylinders.

Whether they were big or small, the firecrackers were all Yankee Boys. On the label, two boys wearing striped shirts and shorts lit a string of firecrackers. A huge pagoda watched safely from a distant hilltop.

The red tissue paper of my packets rustled in my hands. But I was still feeling bad about Uncle's watch. Uncle had given up too much to help me out.

When all of us had firecrackers, Uncle made sure everyone knew the rules because firecrackers are dangerous. Never hold a lit firecracker in your hand. Never stand near a lit one. Never put your face close to a firecracker. And never, never throw a firecracker at anyone or anything.

Then to get things going, Uncle Chester tied strings of ladyfinger firecrackers together. With his cigarette lighter, he touched them off. They exploded like a line of miniature suns along the sidewalk. Each burst sent bits of paper whirling into the air. Gunpowder hovered in ribbons over the spot.

Uncle spread his arms out as wide as he could, as if he wanted to hug the whole world. The flashes cast flickering shadows on his face. Smoke wreathed his grinning face.

"Don't you just love Chinese New Year's?" he shouted over the popping firecrackers. "It's Thanksgiving and Christmas and the Fourth of July all rolled up into fifteen wonderful days. There's lots of food, lots of surprises, and lots of loud fun. So I hope this year is the best ever for everyone!"

The holiday was made for Uncle Chester. He loved family and he loved giving. If Santa Claus meant Christmas, Uncle Chester would always mean Chinese New Year's to me.

We all ripped open our packets then, even Mom and Dad. Pieces of paper littered the sidewalk like tiny red leaves. It was like having a second Christmas.

Uncle Chester had brought along incense sticks. They looked like very dark, skinny Popsicles. The incense was clumped on one end of the stick. After Uncle used his lighter to set a tip on fire, he would hand it to someone. The incense sticks burned slowly.

As the others began lighting their firecrackers with their incense sticks, Uncle came over to me. "You tell me what you want. Then I'll set off your firecrackers for you."

The others' firecrackers banged all around us. Incense mixed with gunpowder smoke.

I tried to hand him my packets. "I don't feel like it. Maybe you can return these. And then save that money to get your watch back."

But Uncle wouldn't take them. "Enjoy what you got while you got it. The watch was great, but, hey"—he raised a shoulder in a shrug—"it just wasn't meant to be permanent."

"Does that apply to people, too?" Mimi asked from behind us.

Uncle gave a nervous laugh. "Of course not."

"You could've fooled me." Mimi sniffed. "Say, have you got the time?"

He tried to bluff his way through. "Aw, my watch's

broken. Can you imagine that?" he asked.

"Why don't you try mine, then?" Mimi asked. She fished Uncle's watch out of her purse. "I happened to find this in a pawnshop and thought you might need it."

"You shouldn't have wasted all that cash," Uncle protested.

"I don't consider it a waste," Mimi said. She took his other wrist and strapped the watch on him. "Have you learned your lesson? Are you going to give up betting on the races?"

Uncle's face filled with pleasure and surprise. He gave Mimi a hug. "For you, yeah."

So Uncle had found something he liked even more than his horses.

"Do you know the Sea Garden?" Mimi asked. That was a fancy Chinese restaurant that had just opened up at Broadway and Grant.

"Sure, but I've never eaten there. I can't afford the prices," Uncle Chester said.

"Well, they need a maître d'," Mimi said.

"What's that?" I asked.

"That's someone who meets you at the door and sits you at a table," Mimi said. "My cousin's the owner. He thinks Chester would be perfect for it since Chester knows everyone in Chinatown."

"I'd like that a lot," Uncle said.

The family couldn't help overhearing everything. And Uncle sheepishly had to explain about pawning the watch and then the good news about the restaurant position.

Everybody thought the new job was ideal for Uncle's talents.

While he was receiving their congratulations, Mimi leaned over to me. "Thanks for telling me, Artie."

"You said it was none of your business, though," I said.

"I thought about it." She gave me a quick peck on the cheek. "And I realized I didn't want to be a stranger to Chester or to you. So thanks. It wouldn't have happened without you."

Maybe I wasn't so useless after all.

Suddenly, I felt like celebrating, so I pointed to my packet of Yankee Boys. "Do you want to help us set off my firecrackers?" Then I remembered. "Oh, you don't like firecrackers, though."

"Your uncle seems to like them a lot," Mimi said,

"so I guess I should too." Then she called to Uncle Chester. "Hey, Chester, give us a hand."

"Yes, ma'am," Uncle said, giving her a salute.

They seemed so happy together, and a little of the happiness was rubbing off on me. I wanted this mood to go on and on.

"Let's make the fun last," I suggested. "Set them off one at a time."

"You're the boss," Uncle said.

Mimi tore the paper from a packet. The ladyfingers' fuses were tied one to the other in a chain. I held the incense stick while she and Uncle untwisted the ladyfingers from one another. Then Mimi placed one on the sidewalk and Uncle touched the incense stick to the fuse.

When it began to sputter, they stepped back quickly.

With a burst of light, a little firecracker exploded like a small star.

Granny clapped her hands. She was sitting on the steps and encouraging everyone. Every now and then she went around giving out curling strips of coconut candy. She said it would help us keep up our strength.

I lost track of time. It seemed as if we were setting off all the firecrackers in the world.

Making noise.

Making light.

Making stars. Not in the night sky, but right here in front of me.

Making stars. Not permanent ones, but short ones that disappeared all too quickly.

Making stars and making people happy. Not forever, but these brief sparkles were the best anyone could do.

Bang. Boom. Bang.

Finally, the last explosion rang in my ears. I was standing ankle deep in red paper. The fuzzy, furry sweetness of the coconut mixed in my mouth with the metallic taste of gunpowder and the perfume of the incense. Thick columns of smoke wriggled around me like a ghostly forest of trees.

I could hear firecrackers still popping in the distance.

"That," Dad said with a sigh, "was really something. Thanks, Artie. Thanks, Chester."

As the others thanked us, Uncle Chester held up his left hand. (Mimi was holding on to his right one.)

"I'll leave the cleanup to the rest of you."

It started to rain. The dragon waited until we were finished before showing up. The downpour would wash away the debris. So we didn't have to clean up. Dragons really brought good luck.

"Come inside." Granny beckoned to Mimi. "I'll make up a special plate for you."

Tired but glad, we followed her into our cousins' home.

There was a carnival that wedged itself into Waverly Place a few days before the official parade. I turned to Mimi. "Do you want to go to the carnival when it comes?

"Sure," she said. "Count me in." Then she glanced at Uncle. "Want to tag along, Chester?"

"I guess." Uncle smiled.

Uncle's wish came true. It was the best year for everyone, especially for him and Mimi. And Uncle was *really* good at his new job. A few months later, he and Mimi got married.

At their wedding, there were plenty of firecrackers. Just like a whole galaxy of stars bursting.

AFTERWORD

The customs portrayed in this book are from my family's ancestral area, southern China. While my family did not follow many of the old traditions, my grandparents did insist on certain ones, especially at Chinese New Year's.

We weren't allowed to play with toy guns or quarrel with one another. And my grandmother prepared all the food before the first day of the New Year so she wouldn't have to use a knife and accidentally cut up the family's luck. We also ate lots of the noodle dish *jai*, and, having been a spoiled, greedy brat, the first Chinese I would have learned was *Goong hay fat choy* and *li see*.

To write this story, I've drawn on my own memories of Chinatown back then, including the frenzy at a fruit stand that I've called the Happy Paradise. My walks with my grandmother or my Auntie Mary could take as long as Artie's with Uncle Chester.

While there are some differences between the regions of China, traditionally, the Chinese New Year's celebration lasts for fifteen days, with specific things to be done on each day.

However, before the New Year started, each household would want to preserve as much of its luck as it could. So families cleaned their houses before New Year's began so that none of their good fortune might be swept away by mistake, along with the dust and clutter, during the actual New Year. For decoration, they would also hang up happy wishes and blessings and short poems written on strips of red paper.

In addition, at the end of the year, people would try to pay their debts and send the Kitchen God up to Heaven to make his report. People also got haircuts before New Year's because, again, scissors and razors might cut some of their luck.

Every home would have had some flowers, as well. Because plum trees flower in the winter, their blossoms have come to stand for many things, like courage, determination, hope, and trustworthiness. Peach tree blossoms symbolize immortality as well as the coming of spring, but in San Francisco, where there aren't any peach trees, people use quince blossoms instead. Because the narcissus always blooms at this time of year, it has also found its way into Chinese homes as a sign of luck.

On one of the tables would be some fresh fruit, like oranges, because the Chinese word for orange sounds like the Chinese word for good fortune. There would also be a box or dish with eight sections. In every section would be a different type of treat, each with its own symbolism, including slices of candied melon, which represent health, and sugary strips of white coconut, which symbolize family unity. Dyed melon seeds signify virtue.

On New Year's Eve, families would gather for a meal together just as Artie's does. They would have the *jai* dish as well as a fish complete with head and tail. That's because the Chinese word for fish (*yu*) is also a pun on the word for abundance. The chicken, cooked with its feet and head, would symbolize completeness and family unity. Noodles would be served uncut to represent long life.

In the old days, to scare away evil spirits on New Year's Eve, storekeepers would set off firecrackers in front of their businesses, and families would do the same in front of their homes. For the sake of the neighbors, our family set off firecrackers on the first day of the New Year rather than at midnight on New Year's Eve.

In the morning of the first day of New Year's, a traditional family would pay its respects to its ancestors if it had a shrine in its home. Then the children would wish luck and prosperity to their parents and older family members, who would reciprocate by handing out *li see*, red envelopes with new coins or even dollar bills. In some families, the wish giving was done on New Year's Eve.

Sometime during the same day, people might have gone to the temple to offer food to the gods and have their fortunes told for the New Year. There, it was also possible to burn special currency and send it to the dead along with paper cutouts of other things a loved one might need in the afterlife.

The Chinese follow a cycle of twelve years. Each year is associated with an animal. They are, in order: the rat, the ox, the tiger, the rabbit, the dragon, the snake, the horse, the ram, the monkey, the rooster, the dog, and the pig. There are various stories about how that order was determined. In one tale, Heaven held a race to decide the matter. Clever Rat asked Ox to carry him, and good-natured Ox agreed. Somehow Ox managed to gallop past the other creatures, but as he neared the finish line, Rat jumped off from his head and across the line ahead of everyone else. That's why the rat is the first year of the Chinese zodiac.

Since I was born in the Year of the Rat, my brother sometimes teased me about being a rat. However, I take pride in the fact that children born in the Year of the Rat are said to be clever. Uncle Chester was born in 1924, which makes him a rat like me. Artie was born in 1945, which makes him a rooster.

Children born in certain years have qualities associated with the animal that represents their year. To learn more about the Chinese zodiac, please consult the partial bibliography at the end of this book.

In San Francisco, the Chinese New Year parade with the dragon and the floats actually occurs after the main festivities are over. During New Year's itself, people are too busy with their families and friends to work on such an elaborate project. When I was a boy, the parade went down Grant Avenue, the heart of Chinatown, but even then the crowds were already growing too large for that narrow space. For safety concerns, the parade route was moved elsewhere.

PARTIAL BIBLIOGRAPHY

P lease be careful when using sources on the internet, as they don't always distinguish between Chinese regions.

Listed below are some of the books that I used in writing this story:

Delsol, Paula. *Chinese Astrology*. Translated from the French by Peter and Tanya Leslie. New York: Warner Books, 1972.

Hu, William C. *Chinese New Year: Fact and Folklore*. Ann Arbor, Michigan: Ars Ceramica, 1992.

Lau, Theodora. *Handbook of Chinese Horoscopes*. New York: Harper & Row: 1979.

Sun, Ruth Q. *The Asian Animal Zodiac*. Rutland, Vermont: Charles E. Tuttle, 1974.

DATE DUE